CW00516935

# My First Songbook

# Melanie Cossins

To the best of our knowledge all the songs and rhymes in this book are in the common domain, being a part of the oral tradition of being passed down from teacher to pupil over many generations. Should we have failed to acknowledge any copyright material please contact us immediately.

Copyright 2020 Melanie Cossins

My First Songbook
All rights reserved
Melanie Cossins, Wakefield, UK

ISBN: 978-1-913951-00-9

www.cossinsmusicschool.co.uk

@Melicos

# Contents

I hope that you enjoy My First Songbook. Repetition of these songs is very important for musical memory for both you and your child. Have fun singing and playing with your child as well as enjoy singing for yourself.

Singing has many benefits for health and well-being including helping breathing, releasing stress and anxiety and raising dopamine levels (related to feelings of happiness).

We feel music throughout our bodies as well as through our ears and visually. Anytime you sing with your baby, tap the pulse (using the heartbeats as a guide) on your child's body or use a movement like rocking to help them feel the *pulse*. Throughout the book there are ideas for activities to accompany each song, these suit different ages and stages of your child's development. With older children, you may just like to sing the songs and tap the heart beats on the pages in time with the *pulse*.

Have fun and enjoy singing!

*Melanie x*

Find Cossins Music School on Facebook, Twitter, Soundcloud, YouTube and Instagram.

I firmly believe that singing is extremely important to a child's development.

***Did you know unborn babies can hear sound at around 20 weeks?***
Tapping into that unborn musicality is a great place to start!

Children can learn so much from singing and music learning: new words, sentence structures, intonation, rhythmic patterns, counting – these are just a few! They also become more confident learners and better listeners through participating in musical activities – much more so than any other activity! This is because music activates all parts of the brain.

Music training in the early years can give your child a firm base and understanding of musical concepts through singing and playing fun games.

Kodály's approach to music learning is based on teaching, learning and understanding music through song. Singing gives everyone access to music without any technical know-how of playing an instrument. Our voice is our very own instrument!

Engaging in singing has been shown to:

⭐ Build confidence.

⭐ Give people a sense of unity (it is something everyone can do despite race, age, ability, social and economic factors etc).

⭐ Improve feelings of joy and sociability.

⭐ Increase levels of concentration, achievement and social harmony.

# Singing helps children's....

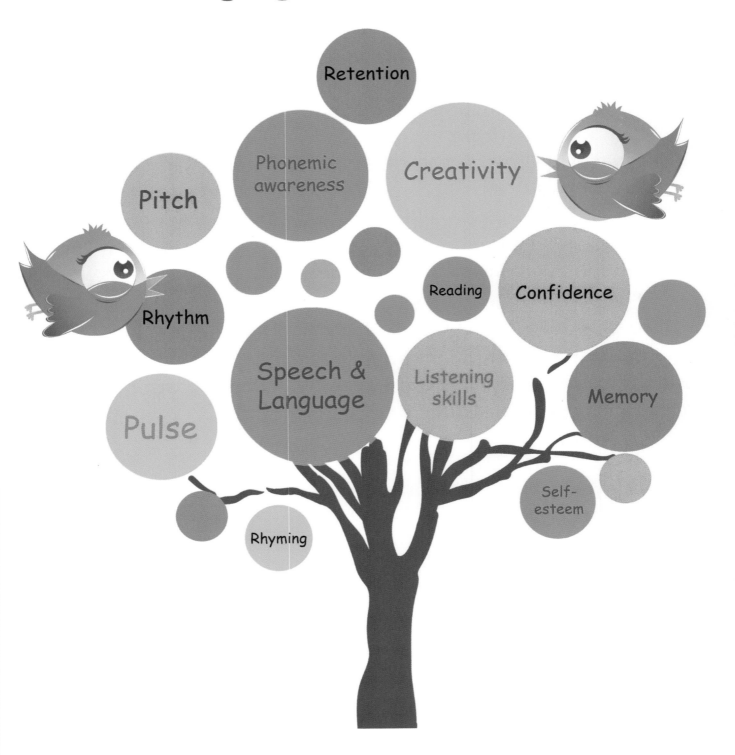

# Why singing games and rhymes are important

Research has shown that singing and rhymes with movement have an extremely positive effect on children's development.

**Singing with your child can help:**

 Develop speech: songs and rhymes are pronounced more clearly because the speech is slower and easier for a child to imitate. The rhythms in song and rhyme help patterns and phrases of speech.

 Increase your child's understanding of language: research has shown that a greater knowledge of nursery rhymes improves a child's phonetical awareness and this will help them be a more fluent reader.

 Develop memory and retention skills: A child is able to memorise easily through the constant repetition of rhymes and songs.

 Emotional skills: intellectual skills are linked to a child's emotional growth.

 Develop motor skills and co-ordination: clapping, stamping and moving to music helps develop gross and fine motor skills.

 Enhance listening skills: your child is concentrating on the song/rhyme and is focusing on you and will respond more to instructions.

 Social skills: singing encourages your child to communicate with you at an early stage by making babbling sounds.

**PULSE:** the "heartbeat" of a song or piece of music. It is a regular unit of time. Follow the heartbeats pictured along with the songs and rhymes in this book.

**RHYTHM:** a pattern of sounds that are long, short or of equal duration. Clapping the words of the songs in this book is the rhythm.

**PITCH:** how high or low a sound is. Pitch matching is the ability to sing back a melody exactly the same as it is sung.

**DYNAMICS:** the volume of sound - louder and quieter.

**TEMPO:** the speed of the song or music - faster and slower.

**POLYPHONIC HEARING:** the ability to hear two or more melodies simultaneously (the basis of harmonic hearing).

**REST:** the gaps (silence) in the music where nothing is played. This is called a musical rest. You will see this in the book represented by this symbol (Z)

**RHYMES:** are spoken using our "speaking voice"

**SONGS:** are sung using our "singing voice"

# Roll the Ball

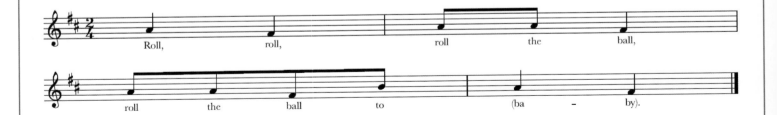

soundcloud.com/melanie-cossins/rolltheball

# Roll, roll, roll the ball,

# roll the ball to (ba-by).

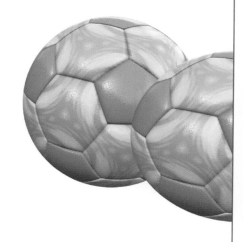

**Babies:**
Lay your baby on the floor and rock them from side to side to the *pulse* (the heartbeats) as you sing. You can change the word 'baby' to the name of your child. If you have another adult you could roll a ball back and forth sitting down whilst one of you holds your baby between your legs or play together with another parent and their baby. Remember to sing the name of the baby as you roll the ball towards them. Balls with good texture or bells inside are great for engaging tiny babies. Older babies sitting up can sit opposite you as you roll, encourage them to roll the ball back to you. Try rolling a ball around the room as your baby chases after it.

**Toddlers:**
Sit opposite your toddler an encourage your toddler to catch the ball from you. Sing the song first using their name and then roll the ball. Sing again and sing your name or 'mummy', 'daddy' etc.
You could also sing and tap the balls on this page in time with the *pulse*.

**Preschoolers:**
Use the same game as for toddlers however you can sing roll the ball, bounce the ball or even throw the ball using the corresponding action.
Sing and tap the balls on this page in time with the *pulse* as you sing. Can your child do it by themselves? Count the balls – how many are there? There are eight (there are eight beats in this song!)

# Hey Ho

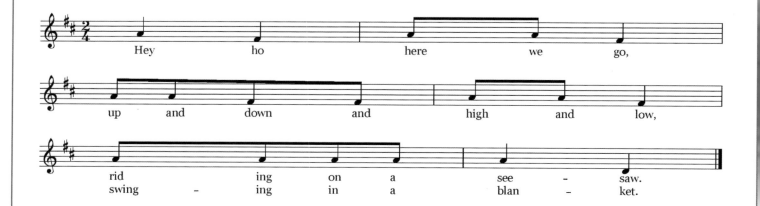

soundcloud.com/melanie-cossins/heyho

# Hey Ho here we go,

## up and down and high and low,

### Rid-ing on a see saw.

## (Swing-ing in a blan-ket)

### Babies:

Sit on the floor with your legs stretched out and your baby laying on your knee. Rock your baby from side to side in time with the *pulse* (the heartbeats) – tiny babies can be rocked in your arms. When your baby is sitting you can sit them on your legs and lift your knees up and down in time with the *pulse* and *pitch* of the song (high, low, high low etc)- this will give them the feeling of moving up and down as you sing high and low pitches.

If you feel brave, put your baby in a blanket or towel and with a partner, swing them from side to side – babies love the rocking sensation.

### Toddlers:

Sit on the floor opposite your toddler and hold hands. Rock from side to side in time with the *pulse* (the heartbeats). If you are feeling energetic, sit on your knees and let your toddler stand on your knees while holding their hands and let them sway forwards and backwards. If you have a see-saw rocker or are at the park, let them sit on the see saw and rock them in time with the *pulse* as you sing the song.

### Preschoolers:

Sit on the floor with your arms stretched out either side. As you sing, let one hand touch the floor at one side whilst the other goes up in the air and pretend to be a see saw, as you rock from side to side. You could also do this standing and sway from foot to foot lifting the other off the ground. Balance boards are great for physical development: let your child stand on the board and hold hands with you. As you sing help your child move the board so that it touches the ground on each side in time with the *pulse* and with the *pitch*.

# Mary Ann

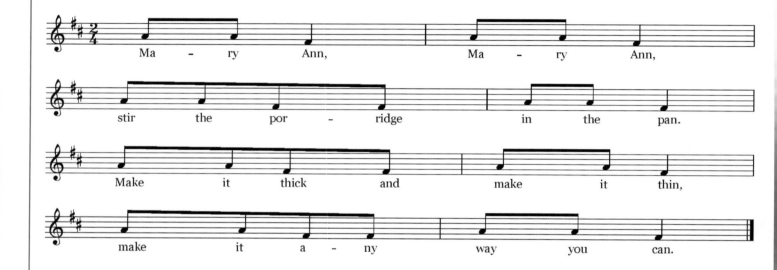

Ma - ry Ann, Ma - ry Ann,

stir the por - ridge in the pan.

Make it thick and make it thin,

make it a - ny way you can.

soundcloud.com/melanie-cossins/maryann

Ma-ry Ann, Ma-ry Ann,

♥     ♥     ♥     ♥

stir the por-ridge in the pan,

♥     ♥     ♥     ♥

make it thick and make it thin,

♥     ♥     ♥     ♥

make it an-y-way you can.

♥     ♥     ♥     ♥

### Babies:
Sit your baby on your knee and as you sing the song move your baby around in a clockwise direction (as if stirring some porridge) older babies you can hold their hands and pretend to stir. Do a full rotation taking two heartbeats. Repeat going anti-clockwise. Sing the song and also bounce your baby in time with the heartbeats. Try singing faster and slower, quiet and loud.

### Toddlers:
Keeping toddlers interested usually requires props. Find a pan and a spoon from your cupboard and pretend stirring the pan as you sing – try to stir in time with the *pulse*. You might like to put something in the pan such as balls or wooden bricks! Balls work well as toddlers like to try and balance them on the spoon! Try getting them to stir with different hands helping cross the mid-line.

### Preschoolers:
Sitting on the floor tell your child you are making porridge and can they help stir it. Imagine you have a big pan, as you sing, pretend to stir with one hand in a clockwise direction repeat the song and stir anti-clockwise. Swap hands and repeat. Ask how you could make it thicker (your child may say add more oats) -as it is thicker it is harder to stir so this time sing slowly using both hands. Now it is too thick! How could we make it thinner? By adding more milk! Repeat the above action but sing faster. Oops you've spilled some on your knee! - pat your knees in time with the *pulse* (whilst singing) to wipe it away. Maybe there is some on your shoulders, head or somewhere else! You can wipe it off your child and them pretend to wipe it off you! Make sure you do this whilst singing the song and following the heartbeats. Maybe it went on the floor too!
Add things to the porridge – raisins, honey, sugar, strawberries -whatever your child likes! Have a taste!
Tap the heartbeats as you sing. How many heartbeats are there?(sixteen) – this means there are sixteen beats in this song.

Chop, chop, chop-pit-y chop,

Chop off the bot-tom and chop off the top,

What we have left we will put in the pot,

Chop, chop, chop-pit-y chop!

**Stir it round, stir it round
taste and see what you have found!**

**Babies:**
With your baby speak the rhyme and bounce them on your knee using the heartbeats to guide you for the *pulse*. Try tapping different parts of your baby's body such as feet, tummy, legs etc as you say the words. With older babies, hold their hand out and using the side of your hand make a chopping motion as you say the rhyme. When speaking the 'stir it round' part, roll your baby around on your knee (if sitting) or if laying down use their legs and move them around in a circle as if stirring. Remember to use lots of intonation in your voice as you say this rhyme!

**Toddlers:**
Sitting down first show your toddler the chopping action by holding one hand out flat with palm up, whilst using the other side of your hand to make a chopping action. You can talk about different vegetables, pretend to chop them up how you make soup. Older toddlers might like to try the preschool idea below.

**Preschoolers:**
Sit down and tell your child you have a big pot and you are going to make a vegetable soup (you can vary this and have other types of soup e.g. a witches soup - frogs, bats etc)
Ask your child what vegetable they would like to put in - let's say potatoes. You then ask what size potato? Big, medium or tiny! Vary the words for description e.g. Ginormous, huge, small etc. Most of the time children will want ginormous vegetables so it maybe an idea to only give them a couple of options for variety.

Let's say they pick to have a big potato. You then ask them what to cut it with? They will probably say knife, however you can ask them whether a knife will get through this big a potato and see if they can come up with other ideas (maybe axes, swords, saws, scissors etc). As you say the rhyme chop your vegetable in time with the pulse using the action of the chosen tool. At the end of the rhyme you then scoop it all up and put it in the pot saying the "stirring" rhyme as you stir the pot – pretend to have a taste! Yum!

# Here I  am,(z)

♥    ♥  ♥    ♥

# Lit-tle (jump-ing) Joan.(z)

♥      ♥        ♥    ♥

# When no-bod-y's with me,

♥    ♥        ♥    ♥

# I'm all a-lone.(z)

♥    ♥    ♥    ♥

**Babies:**
Sit your baby on your knee and as you say the rhyme use two fingers and pretend to jump a 'Joan' on your baby's knees, toes, tummy, head, shoulders – any part of the body. Keep in time with the *pulse* shown by the heartbeats. You may also like to bounce older babies on your knee or if beginning to stand jump them on the floor (make sure you support them by holding them around the chest, under the arms).

**Toddlers:**
Your toddler will want to try jumping – you can support them under the arms if they need help. Pile up some cushions on the floor and try jumping on those whilst saying the rhyme or use a trampoline and anything bouncy!

**Preschoolers:**
Your preschool child may have ideas of their own you can encourage them to think for themselves and be creative. Start by jumping and then ask them for another action to do instead of jumping. e.g clapping, stamping, swinging arms, tapping head – you can then change the word "jumping" to what ever action you are doing. Try and keep the action to the *pulse* of the rhyme. Jump your finger on the heartbeats as you sing.

# Bum-ble bee, Bum-ble bee,

# Stung a man u-pon his knee

# Stung a pig u-pon his snout

# Good-ness me I think you'-re out!

**Babies:**
Use this rhyme for bouncing or tapping parts of your baby's body. Sitting your baby on your knee bounce them in time with the *pulse* (the bees) as you say the rhyme and on the word out drop them between your legs. You can also do this as a rocking motion and then a dropping motion in your arms. Tap different parts of your baby's body, feet, knees, nose, head etc as you repeat the rhyme.

**Toddlers:**
With your toddler tap different parts of their body using two fingers, you could use a bee puppet or make something to attach to your fingers. Using the bee puppet you can pretend to land the bee puppet on the different parts of their body and repeat the rhyme. Don't forget bees make a buzzing sound as they fly to the different body parts!

**Preschoolers:**
With a bee puppet ask your child to hold their hands out together, palms up – they could cup these to make a flower shape. Using the bee puppet tap your child's hand in time with the *pulse*. Your child may like to hold a bee puppet on their own fingers and tap different parts of their body or you can follow the idea above for toddlers.
Repeat the rhyme and see if they can catch the bee on the word 'out'! See if you can say the rhyme whilst tapping the bees on this page. Count the bees – how many are there? There are sixteen beats in this rhyme! Which other song has the same number? (Mary Ann, Bell Horses, Chop Chop, Jumping Joan etc)

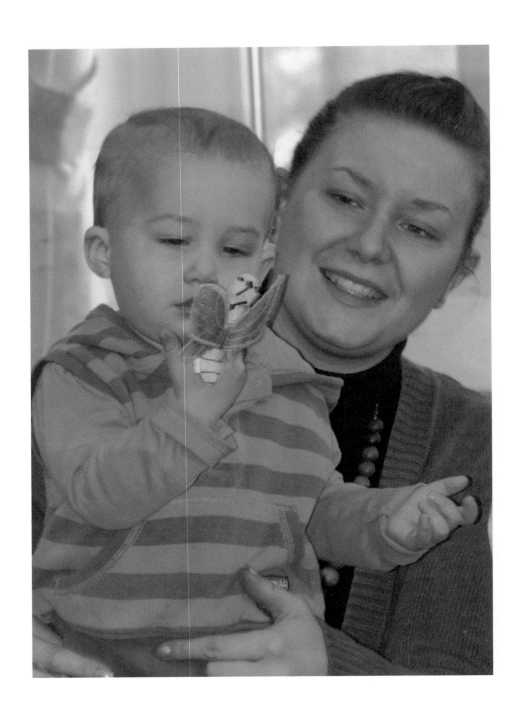

## Action song: Flutter, Flutter Butterfly

# Flut-ter, flut-ter but-ter-fly

# Flut-ter off in-to the sky

# Flut-ter, flut-ter ve-ry fast

# Wave to me as you go past

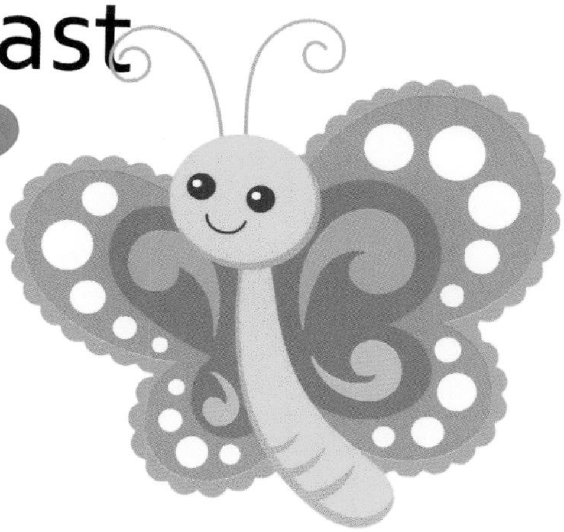

# Bye, bye but-ter-fly!

**Babies & Toddlers**
Using your hands to form a butterfly (hands flat out in front of you – palms down, thumbs touching) as you say the rhyme move your hands, flapping them up and down, in time with the *pulse* (the heartbeats) in an upwards motion.

On the third line flap your hands high above your head in time with the syllables of the words (this is the *rhythm*).

On the fourth line wave your hands again to the *pulse*.

On the last line make your butterfly hands again and on the last heartbeat hide your hands behind your back! This is like a peek-a-boo type game and your toddler will want to copy you!

**Preschoolers:**
You may want to encourage more movement to this rhyme by asking your child to use their arms as wings (you can also use scarves) – perhaps they could hide behind something or curl up on the very last heartbeat? You could also use this rhyme to play a hide and seek game – this could work with toddlers too!

# The Birdies Fly Away

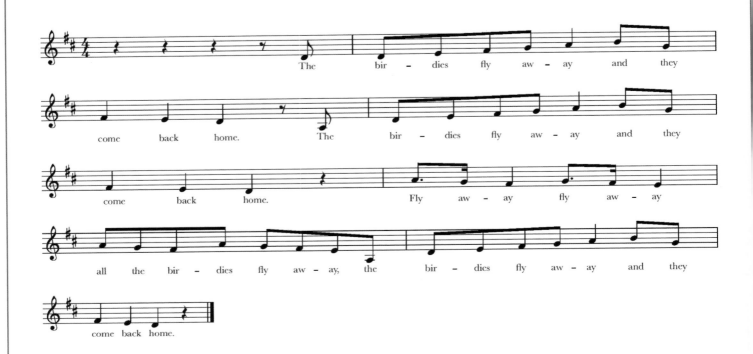

soundcloud.com/melanie-cossins/thebirdiesflyaway

The / bird-ies fly a-way and they

♥      ♥     ♥    ♥

Come back home (z), The

♥      ♥     ♥     ♥

bird-ies fly a-way and they

♥      ♥     ♥     ♥

Come back home (z)

♥      ♥     ♥     ♥

Fly a-way, fly a-way

♥      ♥     ♥    ♥

all the birdies fly a-way, The

♥      ♥     ♥     ♥

bird-ies fly a-way and they

♥      ♥     ♥     ♥

Come back home (z)

♥      ♥     ♥     ♥

## Babies:

Lay your baby in front of you. Facing your baby, using your hands to be the birds, wave or wiggle them in front of your baby and as you sing the first line, slowly move them behind your back and hide them away. On the second line bring them back in front of you and on the word 'home' tickle your baby's tummy. On lines five and six move your hands up high in front of your so your baby can see and repeat the actions as in lines one and two for the last two lines of the song. You could also use a puppet.

## Toddlers:

Find a spot that will be 'home' - you could use a mat as a visual reference. With young toddlers starting at 'home', as you sing pick them up in your arms and fly away from 'home' making sure you return to the spot exactly on the word 'home' (see below for older toddlers).

## Preschoolers:

Similar to toddlers find a place to call 'home' or your nest. As you sing pretend to be birds using your arms to fly. As you sing the song, fly away from your 'home' but try and encourage your child to only return to their starting place on the word 'home'. You can emphasise this by jumping on the spot you have called 'home'. If you have some scarves you could use them as wings.
Try singing the song slower and faster. Great fun!

# Snail, Snail / Mouse, Mouse

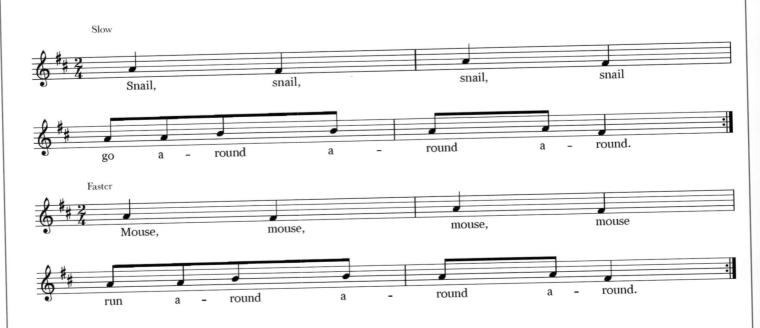

soundcloud.com/melanie-cossins/snailsnail

Sing slowly

# Snail, snail, snail, snail,

♥  ♥  ♥  ♥

# go a-round, a-round, a-round.

♥  ♥  ♥  ♥

Sing faster

# Mouse, mouse, mouse, mouse,

♥  ♥  ♥  ♥

# run a-round, a-round, a-round.

♥  ♥  ♥  ♥

**Babies:**
Singing the song, bounce your child to the *pulse* using the heartbeats to guide you. Make sure you sing the 'snail..' song slowly and the 'mouse' song faster. With young babies lay them on the floor and walk your fingers up your baby's arms or legs and give them a tickle at the end.
You can also do this carrying your baby and tapping them or as you walking the *pulse* yourself, moving slow and fast as you sing the corresponding song.

**Toddlers:**
This is a great song to encourage your toddler to move. Sometimes getting to and from places can be difficult! Try this song to see who can get somewhere the fastest and also being the slowest (this is encouraging a feel for *Tempo*). Make sure you encourage walking to the *pulse,* as you sing the 'mouse' version and as you sing the faster 'mouse' song your movements will be quicker as the *pulse* becomes faster. Alternate between the two songs.

**Preschoolers:**
Follow the ideas above for 'Toddlers' however you can ask your child to join hands with you as you walk or jog weave in and out of objects in your environment and around to add variation. If you have several children you can all join hands making a line.

29

# Bell Horses

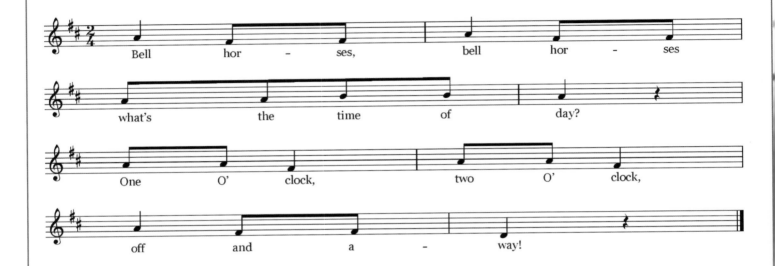

Bell hor - ses, bell hor - ses

what's the time of day?

One O' clock, two O' clock,

off and a - way!

soundcloud.com/melanie-cossins/bellhorses

# Bell hor-ses, bell hor-ses,

♥ ♥ ♥ ♥

# What's the time of day? (z)

♥ ♥ ♥ ♥

# One o'clock, two o'clock,

♥ ♥ ♥ ♥

# Off and a-way! (z)

♥ ♥ ♥ ♥

**Babies:**
Lay your baby on the floor and as you sing tap their body to the *pulse* on the very last beat marked with a (Z) lift their legs up in the air. If your baby is older sit them on your knee facing away from you hold their feet and tip them backwards towards you lifting their feet and legs. As your baby gets older they will love to be bounced and lifted in the air, so sit them on your knee as you sing the song bounce them in time with the *pulse*. On the very last beat, lift you baby high in the air. Try singing this song faster and slower (*Tempo*), quiet and loud (*Dynamics*)

**Toddlers:**
Children who are walking can play the following game with you. Stand at one end of a room (or outside space) as you sing tap your legs in time with the *pulse*. On the last beat (Z) run as fast as you can to the other side. Try and get your child to wait until the very last beat! They will love trying to run as fast as they can. Try singing this and shaking some bells.

**Preschoolers:**
Preschoolers will still love the game above however they must listen and wait for the very end of the song. They will love the competitive element of trying to beat you in a race! You could also have a designated place that is the 'stable' and the horses are to return to the stable when you sing "five o'clock, six o'clock, home for today" replacing the 3rd and 4th lines above. Great for listening skills and anticipating the end of the song – meaning your child is thinking ahead of time.

# Peter Taps

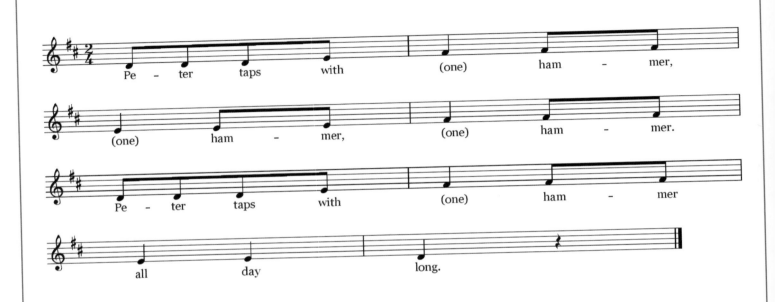

soundcloud.com/melanie-cossins/petertaps

# Pe-ter taps with (one) ham-mer,

# (one) ham-mer, (one) ham-mer.

# Pe-ter taps with (one) ham-mer,

# all day long. (z)

**\*Remember you can use this song to count up e.g. two hammers, three hammers up to five.**

## Babies:

As you sing the song tap the *pulse* (marked with the shoe and hammer) on your babies feet. Tap one foot then repeat on the other foot. You can do this with them lying down or sitting facing away from you in your lap. Now try tapping both their feet together, making sure the soles of the feet meet – bend your baby's knees to get the soles of their feet together. When you tap on your child's body they internalise *pulse* physically whilst hearing the song.

## Toddlers:

Toddlers love having a go at things themselves so find a drum with a beater or a toy hammer and encourage your toddler to 'hammer' in time with the *pulse*. If you gently tap them whilst they are playing they will feel this through their body. Older toddlers could have a go with shoes like preschoolers.

## Preschoolers:

Preschoolers can have lots of fun with their shoes. Both you and your child put a shoe on one hand and make a fist with the other (as a 'hammer'). Turn your shoe over so that the sole is pointing upwards and as you sing use your fist to tap on the shoe to the *pulse*. You could also see if they can think of any other shoe actions like wiping the dirt off their shoe, polishing, mending their shoe: stitching, gluing the sole on etc. See if they can follow the shoe and hammer pictures and tap each one in turn as you sing. Play the game where you start with one foot, then add the other, then hand tapping leg, then other hand tapping as well and last of all adding your head – for the fifth hammer.

# Nenne

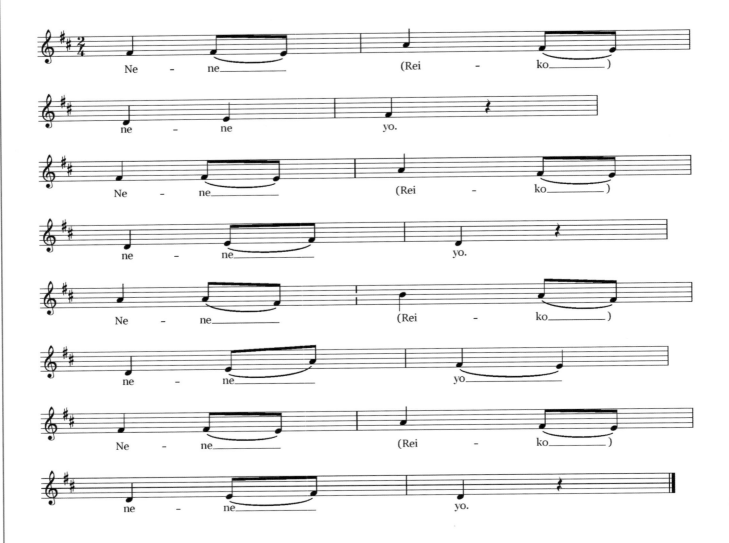

soundcloud.com/melanie-cossins/nenne

# Nen-ne, (Rei-k-o), Nen-ne yo   (z)

# Nen-ne, (Rei-k-o), Nen-ne yo   (z)

# Nen-ne, (Rei-k-o), Nen-ne yo__

# Nen-ne, (Rei-k-o), Nen-ne yo   (z)

## Babies:
This is a beautiful Japanese lullaby, the word Reiko is a Japanese girls name. Rock your baby gently as you sing using the heartbeats to guide you. Make sure you sing your baby's name as you rock. You could also stroke their hair or pat them gently as you sing.

## Toddlers:
With toddlers you could rock a doll or teddy bear or just lay on the floor whilst you sing. Stroking hair or gently patting on the heartbeats is a lovely way to get them to feel the *pulse* whilst also having lovely parent-child time. A lovely lullaby to sing your child to sleep with.

## Preschoolers:
You could do as with toddlers above and change the name 'Reiko' to their name your name, mummy, daddy etc. You could also rock teddy/doll in a blanket or scarf. Try rock to the *pulse* using the heartbeats.

Mel has been teaching music to children for over fifteen years and built up a wealth of experience working with parents and young children, nurseries, junior & infants as well as adults. She runs early years music sessions both privately and in nurseries; teaches vocals, recorder and ukulele to children and adults; leads adult mental health and well-being singing groups and sessions for vulnerable teenagers. She has also worked with Wakefield Theatre Royal Performance Academy as a singing tutor.

Mel has attended many Kodály training courses and now works using this philosophy. In 2017 she travelled to Budapest in Hungary (home of Zoltán Kodály) to visit their nurseries where the Kodály philosophy is still practiced, and music is an essential part of their education system. She was lucky to have training from one of the top Hungarian Kodály tutors Helga Dietrich whilst there, visit Kodály's home and the Kodály music institute in Kecskemét.

In 2017 Mel secured substantial funding from Wakefield Council Culture Cures to run creative projects for mental health and well-being around the district. In 2018 she co-founded Think Cre8tive Group CIC, and has established programs based around singing and health including a pre/post natal singing group for mums and their babies, Sing It Out! Mama. She has already published several songbooks for Think Cre8tive as well as online audio and visual material.

Singing is a huge part of her life and she truly believes that children benefit hugely from being involved in music making.

Printed in Great Britain
by Amazon

37044709R00023